STORMS

WEATHER REPORT

Ted O'Hare

Rourke
Publishing LLC
Vero Beach, Florida 32964

www.rourkepublishing.com

PHOTO CREDITS: © Wyman Meinzer, pages 10, 15, and 21; South Dakota Tourism, pages 4, 7; NASA, pages 8, 13, and 17; © Lynn M. Stone, pages 12, 18

Title page: *Lightning bolts dance over the Badlands of western South Dakota.*

Series Editor: Henry Rasof

Cover and interior design by Nicola Stratford

Library of Congress Cataloging-in-Publication Data

O'Hare, Ted, 1961-
  Storms / Ted O'Hare.
     v. cm. — (Weather report)
Includes bibliographical references and index.
Contents: Storms — Rainstorms — Thunderstorms — Thunder and lightning — Tornadoes — Hurricanes — Blizzards — Icy storms — Predicting storms.
  ISBN 1-58952-572-8 (hardcover)
  1. Storms—Juvenile literature. [1. Storms.] I. Title. II. Series.
  QC941.3 .O43 2002
  551.55—dc21
                                                    2002151636

Printed in the USA

CG/CG

Table of Contents

Storms

Sometimes the weather is not sunny. Clouds cover the skies. These days may bring rain and even storms.

Stormy weather brings **precipitation**, usually rain or snow falling from the sky. And it may bring strong winds.

Storms may cause damage to buildings, roads, and crops. Storms may knock down power lines. Storms may injure and even kill people.

Fast-moving thunderstorms, like this one in South Dakota, can create deadly tornadoes.

Rainstorms

Some people call them "trash movers" or "gully washers." Mostly they're called rainstorms. They can be dangerous when they cause **flooding**.

Flooding happens when the ground cannot soak up the rain fast enough. This might happen when the ground is very dry. Flooding also happens when streams or rivers are already full of water. They overflow their banks because the rain has no place to go.

Flooding leaves even normally dry land under water.

Thunderstorms

Thunderstorms are loud storms with wind, lightning, and rain. A thunderstorm happens in steps. First the sun heats the ground, forcing warm, wet air to rise. Then the warm air meets colder, drier air. Finally, **thunderclouds** form.

These thunderclouds can produce heavy rain. And sometimes the rain in the clouds moves upward into cooler air. Then the raindrops form balls of ice called hail.

Clouds called thunderheads build up over Southeast Asia in a view taken from the Space Shuttle.

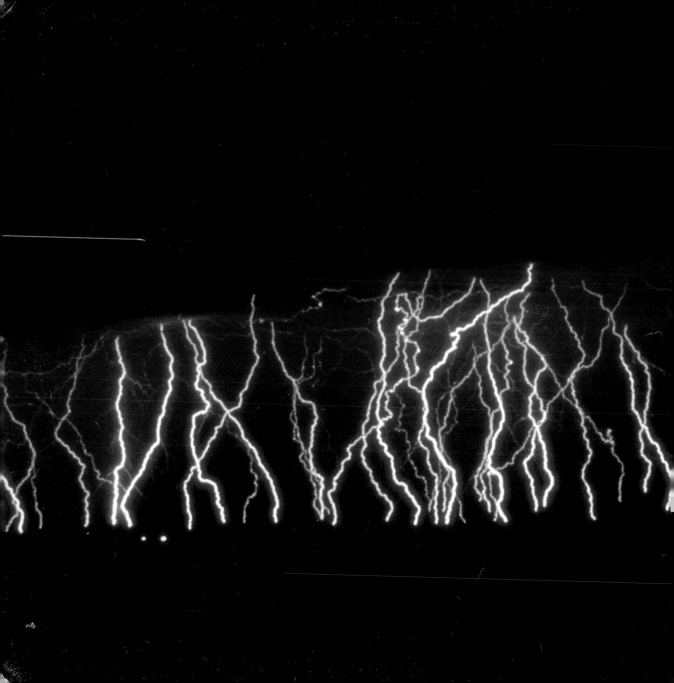

Thunder and lightning

Every thunderstorm contains electricity called lightning. Some thunderstorms contain a great deal of lightning.

Bolts of lightning may travel between clouds or inside clouds. Or they may travel between a cloud and the ground. When lightning strikes the ground, there can be great danger.

Heat produced by lightning makes the air around it very hot. This heated air explodes outward, creating thunder. Thunder may be loud and frightening but is not dangerous.

Lightning can be extremely dangerous if it reaches the ground.

Wind stirs up fine particles of dust and sand in the Nevada desert.

Powerful tropical storms, like this one shown from space, can grow into true hurricanes.

Tornadoes

A **tornado** is a powerful and swirling windstorm. A tornado can develop when winds that move up in a thunderstorm begin to swirl. The winds make a black cloud shaped like a funnel.

As it rushes through the air, a tornado spins like a top. The "tail" of a tornado may touch the ground. When it does, the tail may destroy almost everything that lies in its narrow path.

The tail of a tornado dances toward the ground.

Hurricanes

A **hurricane** is a large storm that begins over the ocean. It is a dangerous storm with high winds and a lot of rain. The hurricane grows in a round shape with a hole in the center. This center is known as the "eye" of the hurricane.

A hurricane's winds range from 74 to well over 100 miles (120 to 160 kilometers) per hour. When a hurricane's winds reach the land, the winds may die down. However, a hurricane's winds can do great damage when they hit land.

This satellite image of Hurricane Bonnie shows its eye in the center.

Blizzards

A **blizzard** is a snowstorm with strong winds. A true blizzard has winds blowing more than 32 miles (50 kilometers) an hour. Along with heavy, blowing snow, a blizzard may bring very cold temperatures.

It may be difficult to walk or drive during a blizzard. Blowing snow hides almost everything in sight. This condition is known as a **whiteout**.

Wolves are suited to withstand the fury of a winter storm.

Icy storms

Hailstorms take place in the summer when pieces of ice hit the ground. Hail is a mix of ice and snow. Hailstones may be as large as baseballs or as small as peas. The largest piece of hail recorded in the United States measured almost 6 inches (15 centimeters) across.

Sleet, which falls during cold weather, is a kind of ice. Freezing rain happens during the winter. It occurs when the ground is much colder than the air. Falling rain turns to ice as it touches the ground.

Falling hailstones can easily damage cars and buildings.

Predicting storms

Weather often changes quickly. This makes it hard to **forecast**, or predict, how the weather will change.

Scientists who study weather are known as **meteorologists**. It is important for these scientists to try to know about storms that may be coming. Knowing when and where storms may hit can save lives and cut down damage.

The National Weather Service tells us what it knows about the chances of dangerous weather. People there use **satellites**, **radar**, and computers to help protect us from storms.

Glossary

blizzard (BLIZ urd) — a driving snowstorm

flooding (FLUHD ing) — when a body of water overflows

forecast (FORE kast) — to predict

hurricane (HER uh kane) — a storm with strong winds and heavy rains

meteorologists (mee tee uh ROL oh jistz) — people who study the weather

precipitation (pree sip uh TAY shun) — rain, snow, and sleet

radar (RAY dahr) — a system in which sound wave echoes are used to locate distant objects in the air

satellites (SAT uh litez) — manmade stations in space, often used to observe weather conditions

thunderclouds (THUN der CLOWDZ) — clouds that produce heavy rain

tornado (tor NAY doh) — a powerful windstorm that swirls

whiteout (WHITE out) — a condition caused by driving snow, in which it is impossible to see almost anything

Index

Further Reading

Cole, Joanna. *The Magic School Bus Inside a Hurricane*. New York: Scholastic, 1995.
Hopping, Lorraine Jean. *Wild Weather: Blizzards*. New York: Scholastic, 1998.
Kramer, Stephen. *Eye of the Storm: Chasing Tornadoes with Warren Faidley*. New York: Putnam's, 1997.

Websites To Visit

www.nhc.noaa.gov/HAW2/english/kids.shtml
www.spc.noaa.gov/faq/tornado/
www.nssl.noaa.gov/edu/

About The Author

Ted O'Hare is an author and editor of children's information books. He divides his time between New York City and a home upstate.

Read · Reason · Write

Bears

Level A
Book 1

Jack Cassidy, Ph.D., and
Drew Cassidy

Illustrated by Pauline Phung
Designed by Kevin Tufarolo

ISBN 0-8454-0105-X
Copyright © 1998 The Continental Press, Inc.

CONTINENTAL PRESS
Elizabethtown, PA 17022

Contents

What This Book Is About

In this book, you will read about six kinds of bears. Three kinds live in North America. Three live in Asia. Look at the map below. Can you find North America? Can you find Asia? Where do you live?

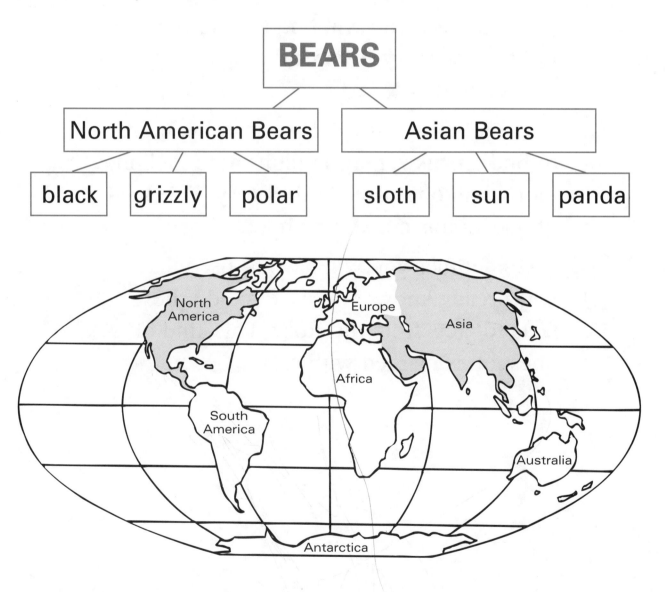

Have fun reading this book about bears!

How to Use This Book

After you read each story, you will see some questions. There are also questions at the end of each part of the book. All the questions will help you understand what you have read.

Sometimes you will find the answers right in the story. This kind of question is marked with a ■.

Sometimes you will have to think more to find an answer. You will have to look in more than one place in the story. This kind of question is marked with a ●.

Sometimes you will have to use what you already know. You have to add these facts to facts from the story. This kind of question is marked with a ★.

In this story, two young black bears learn a lesson.

Black Bear! Black Bear!

① Brownie heard his mother calling. But he did not answer. He and his sister were trying to catch a mouse. They had chased the mouse into a hole. Now they were trying to dig it out.

② Mother bear hurried through the forest. Finally, she saw her children. She rushed up to them. Then she hit each one on the head with her front paws. The young bears were surprised. And they knew their mother was not pleased.

③ Mother bear walked on more slowly. This time, the young bears followed her. At the river, they found a fish and ate it. The bears liked the taste of fish.

④ The bear family crossed the river. Suddenly mother bear was calling out again. This time, the young ones ran straight to her. And then they saw it! It was the biggest bear they had ever seen. It was standing on its back legs. It was showing its huge, sharp teeth!

Mother bear chased her children up the nearest tree. Up they went, as fast as they could. Mother bear climbed up after them.

The big bear was not good at climbing trees. It waited below for a long time. Then it finally went away.

The next time the young black bears saw such a big bear, they would know what to do. Still, it had been a very scary day.

6

Understanding the Story

Here are some questions about the story that you just read. Read each one. Then fill in the circle beside the best answer. If you are not sure, go back and look at the story again.

● 1.   Brownie was

(A)   a mouse

(B)   an old bear

(C)   a black bear

(D)   a grizzly bear

★ 2.   Which sentence tells why the mother bear hit the two young bears?

(E)   They did not come when she called.

(F)   They should not chase a mouse.

(G)   She was afraid of them.

(H)   She was just playing.

■ 3. In the story, the bears ate

(A) a mouse   (C) a seal

(B) a fish   (D) soup

● 4. The story says, "The next time the young black bears saw such a big bear, they would know what to do." They would

(E) run to a cave

(F) jump in the river

(G) hide under a rock

(H) climb a tree

★5. How many bears climbed the tree?

(A) one   (C) three

(B) two   (D) four

● 6. The big bear did not follow the black bears up the tree because it was

(E) not good at climbing

(F) afraid

(G) too tired

(H) not interested in them

Summing Up

What did the two young bears do first? Second? Third? Fourth? Fill in the events in the boxes.

climbed a tree

chased a mouse

ate fish

saw a big bear

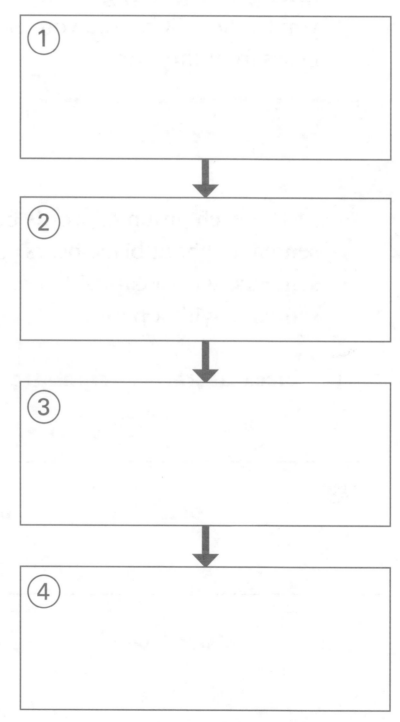

Note to the Writer

Did you know that not all black bears are black? Some are brown. Some are light tan. After you read, it is good to write about what you learned. What did you learn about black bears from the story?

Try This

Use each group of words below and write sentences about black bears. Start each sentence with a capital letter. End each sentence with a period.

black bears   climb trees   fast

1. _____

black bears   eat

2. _____

black bears   are afraid

3. _____

Read • Reason • Write

Pepe saw some grizzly bears. In this letter, he tells his grandma about them.

Pepe and the Grizzly Bears

Dear Grandma,

Do you remember the fish that swim up the stream just once a year? They go up to lay their eggs. The stream is full of them right now. It almost looks silver.

Dad and I went down to the stream to watch the fish. And guess what we saw. Grizzly bears! These animals can get angry quickly. So we did not get too close to them. But we did take pictures. I taped one to the next page for you.

Dad says the bears come to the stream for food. They need to eat lots of fish. The bears must get fat soon. They will sleep all winter.

The young bears stayed on the bank. The older ones jumped into the stream. They caught fish after fish. Then they shared the food with the little bears.

I wish you could have seen them, Grandma.

Love,
Pepe

Understanding the Letter

Here are some questions about the letter that you just read. Read each one. Then fill in the circle beside the best answer. If you are not sure, go back and look at the letter again.

● 1. The letter was mostly about

(A) going fishing

(B) hunting bears

(C) finding silver

(D) watching bears

■ 2. Why was the stream full of fish?

(E) It was always full of fish.

(F) They were going to lay their eggs.

(G) They were trying to get away from the bears.

(H) They had no place else to go.

● 3.   You can tell from the letter that grizzly bears

   (A)   do not like to eat fish

   (B)   can be mean

   (C)   are afraid of water

   (D)   never share their food

■ 4.   The bears must get fat because

   (E)   they don't feel well

   (F)   all bears are fat

   (G)   they will sleep all winter

   (H)   the fish will not last

★5.   Which sentence is a good guess about why only the older bears fished?

   (A)   They wanted all the food.

   (B)   The young ones don't know how yet.

   (C)   The fish were too big.

   (D)   They knew people were around.

★6.   How else could Pepe have told his grandma about the bears?

   (E)   telephone

   (F)   TV

   (G)   radio

   (H)   newspaper

Summing Up

Who did what? Go back to the letter. Find out who did the following things. Write your answers in the blocks.

ate fish.

took pictures.

swam in the river.

Note to the Writer

Some sentences ask questions. These sentences begin with a capital letter. They end with a question mark (?).

Try This

Pretend that you are a grizzly bear. You are catching fish. You see Pepe and his dad watching. Write down some questions that you have about them. Here are some words you could start with.

who   what   where   why   how

1. _____

2. _____

3. _____

4. _____

5. _____

This story is about bears that live far to the north. They are big and white.

A Snowy World

Two little bears were born on a very cold day. At first, they had no fur. Their mother kept them warm. She had made a fine cave in the snow. She slept close to her babies there.

The little bears could not see at first, either. They just stayed inside and drank milk from their mother. But the babies grew fast.

Finally, the bears were big enough to go outside. They found snow and ice all around them. These little bears were polar bears. They lived in the cold Arctic.

By now, the little bears could see very well. They had a white fur coat. But their skin was black.

The mother bear had white fur, too. She even had fur on the bottoms of her feet. Her head was small, and her neck was long. She had very sharp teeth. And she was big. Polar bears are one of the biggest bears of all.

One day, the mother bear took her babies far from home. It was time to hunt. The mother bear had not eaten in a very long time. She walked slowly across the ice. The babies followed her.

Suddenly, the mother stopped. She had seen something. It was a hole in the ice. The big bear sat very still beside the hole. She waited for a long time. Then a seal stuck its head out of the hole. Quickly, the mother bear reached out with her long neck. She grabbed the seal with her sharp teeth. Dinner was ready!

Understanding the Story

Here are some questions about the story that you just read. Read each one. Then fill in the circle beside the best answer. If you are not sure, go back and look at the story again.

■ 1. When polar bears are just born, they have no fur. How do they keep warm?

Ⓐ They grow fur fast.

Ⓑ Their mother keeps them warm.

Ⓒ The father bear holds them.

Ⓓ They come out of the cave.

■ 2. What else is true about baby polar bears?

Ⓔ Their fur is black.

Ⓕ They are always cold.

Ⓖ They do not grow fast.

Ⓗ They cannot see at first.

● 3. Why do you think the mother bear had not eaten in a very long time?

(A) She stayed in the cave with her babies.

(B) She was not hungry.

(C) There was too much food.

(D) She was cold.

★ 4. If you went to the Arctic, you would find

(E) a grass hut

(F) lots of trees

(G) a cold place

(H) no snow

★ 5. A **seal** is

(A) a fish   (C) a bird

(B) an animal   (D) a bear

★ 6. What will the polar bears probably do next?

(E) hunt some more

(F) take a nap

(G) eat the seal

(H) fight over the food

Summing Up

Look at the web. Fill in some facts about polar bears. One circle has already been done for you.

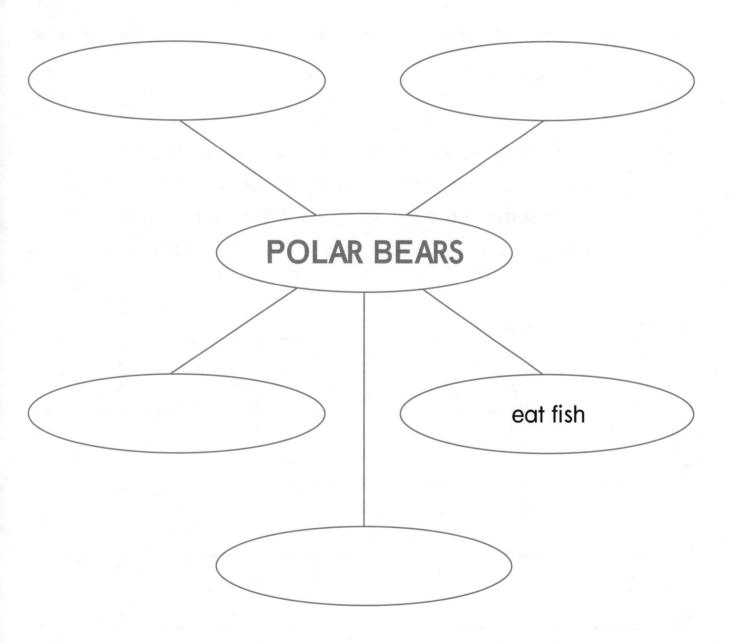

POLAR BEARS

eat fish

Note to the Writer

When you write, you use sentences. Most sentences begin with a capital letter and end with a period.

Try This

Write a sentence for each word or set of words in your polar bear web. Be sure to start each sentence with a capital letter and end it with a period. One sentence is started for you.

1. Polar bears live _____

2. _____

3. _____

4. _____

5. _____

6. _____

Thinking About the Stories

Think about the stories you have read in this part of the book. What do you remember about black bears, grizzly bears, and polar bears? Here are some questions about them. Fill in the circle beside the best answer for each one. If you are not sure, go back and look at the stories again.

● 1. How are all three bears alike?

   Ⓐ They are all the same color.

   Ⓑ They all eat meat or fish.

   Ⓒ They are all the same size.

   Ⓓ They all climb trees.

● 2. How is a polar bear different from a black bear?

   Ⓔ The polar bear is smaller.

   Ⓕ The black bear lives where it is cold.

   Ⓖ The polar bear has white fur.

   Ⓗ The black bear does not like the water.

● 3. In these three bear families, the babies are taken care of by

(A) the father   (C) people

(B) each other   (D) the mother

★4. A big bear chased the black bears. From what you know now, you can guess it might have been

(E) a grizzly bear

(F) another black bear

(G) a polar bear

(H) a zoo bear

● 5. If the big bear was a grizzly, what would be true about grizzly bears?

(A) They are never mean.

(B) They are not good at climbing trees.

(C) They only eat plants.

(D) They are smaller than black bears.

★6. The polar bear is the only one with fur on its feet. What do you think this is for?

(E) killing seals   (G) feeding babies

(F) walking on ice   (H) making a cave

Summing Up

Look at the chart. At the top, there are some facts about bears. Down the side are the names of the bears. Put a + in the box if the fact is true about that bear. Put a — if it is not. The first boxes are done for you.

	has white fur	likes fish	climbs trees
Black Bear	—		
Grizzly Bear	—		
Polar Bear	+		

Note to the Writer

A **caption** is words that tell about a picture. The caption comes right under the picture. A good caption for the picture on page 6 might be

The bears climbed the tree fast.

Try This

Write captions for the other pictures in this part of the book. Then draw a picture of your favorite bear and write a caption for it.

Read • Reason • Write

This story is about the sloth bear. It gets its name from another animal.

Slow and Upside Down

A sloth is an animal that moves very slowly. Sometimes it hangs upside down. The sloth bear is named for this animal. The bear also moves very slowly. And it sometimes hangs upside down.

The sloth bear has a brown and black coat. The hair is long around its shoulders. Baby sloth bears hang from this long hair. That way they can take a ride on their mother. A sloth bear has a white nose. And it has a light **Y** or **U** mark on its dark chest.

Sloth bears cannot see very well. They don't hear very well, either. But they have great noses. These bears can smell things from far away. They can even close their noses whenever they want.

The sloth bear likes to come out at night. It climbs trees to find bird eggs or fruit. It also eats ants, other bugs, and small animals. The sloth bear likes to eat honey, too. In fact, it is sometimes called the honey bear.

Understanding the Story

Here are some questions about the story that you just read. Read each one. Then fill in the circle beside the best answer. If you are not sure, go back and look at the story again.

■ 1. Sloth bears like to come out

    (A) in the morning

    (B) when it rains

    (C) at noon

    (D) at night

● 2. Which of these foods is probably <u>not</u> something that sloth bears eat?

    (E) bird eggs

    (F) rice

    (G) fruit

    (H) bugs

■ 3. Why is the sloth bear sometimes called the honey bear?

   (A) It makes honey.

   (B) It likes to eat honey.

   (C) It is a sweet bear.

   (D) Its fur is sticky.

★4. The word **sloth** is sometimes used to mean

   (E) slow   (G) big

   (F) fast   (H) little

● 5. Which of these can the sloth bear do best?

   (A) hear   (C) smell

   (B) see   (D) run fast

● 6. Why do sloth bears have long hair around their shoulders?

   (E) to keep them warm

   (F) to give their babies a ride

   (G) to hang upside down

   (H) to climb trees

Summing Up

Look at the chart. Then look back at the story. Fill in the missing facts.

SLOTH BEAR

Looks	Eats	Acts
Y or **U** mark	honey	moves slowly

Note to the Writer

When you go to the store, you might have a shopping list. The list tells you what you need to buy.

Try This

Pretend there is a sloth bear grocery store. Make up a shopping list for the sloth bear. Look in the story for ideas.

Sloth Bear Grocery Store
Shopping List

1. __honey_____

2. _____

3. _____

4. _____

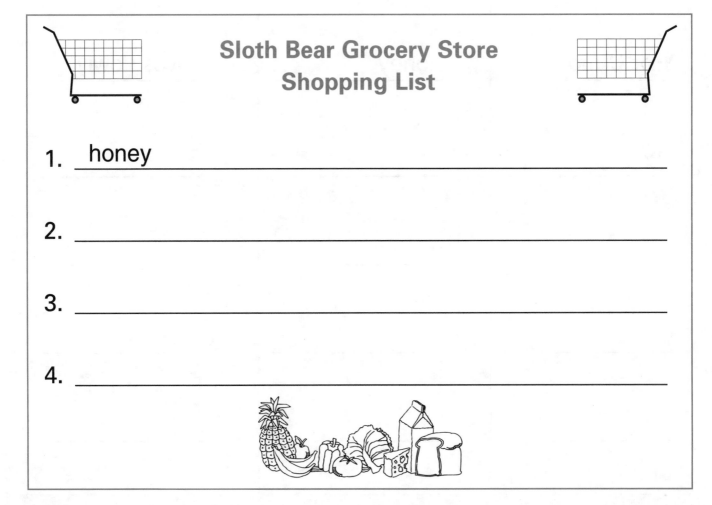

This story is about another bear from Asia. It is the smallest bear in the world.

The Small Bear

The smallest bear in the world is about the size of a child. It is called a sun bear. The sun bear lives in forests in Asia. It has shiny black fur. Its nose is a light color. And it has a patch of white or yellow on its chest.

Not very much is known about sun bears. These animals are afraid of people. So they hide in the forest. They do not come out much during the daytime. It is hard to find them.

Most bears sleep during the winter. The sun bear does not. It does not have to. The weather hardly ever gets cold in its forest home.

The sun bear eats birds and bugs and fruit. Like most bears, it also likes to eat honey.

The smallest bear spends a lot of time up in trees. Of all the bears, the sun bear can climb the best. And it does something in trees that no other bear does. The sun bear makes a bed out of branches and sleeps there! On sunny days, it lies in its nest. It lets the hot sun warm it. Maybe that is why it is called the sun bear.

Read • Reason • Write

Understanding the Story

Here are some questions about the story that you just read. Read each one. Then fill in the circle beside the best answer. If you are not sure, go back and look at the story again.

■ 1. Where does the sun bear live?

   (A) in a hole in the ground

   (B) in a cave

   (C) in forests in Asia

   (D) in a very cold place

■ 2. Which words tell about the sun bear?

   (E) Its fur is soft and white.

   (F) It is hard to find.

   (G) It is very mean.

   (H) It likes to be around people.

● 3.   The sun bear climbs into trees in order to

   (A)   see better

   (B)   eat and sleep

   (C)   get away from other bears

   (D)   look around for a cave

★ 4.   **Branches** are parts of

   (E)   trees

   (F)   houses

   (G)   honey

   (H)   bears

■ 5.   The sun bear is the only bear that

   (A)   climbs trees

   (B)   digs holes

   (C)   eats honey

   (D)   makes a bed in a tree

● 6.   You would probably see a sun bear

   (E)   in the morning

   (F)   after dinner

   (G)   at noon

   (H)   at night

Summing Up

Think about what you know now about sun bears. Fill in some facts in the web below.

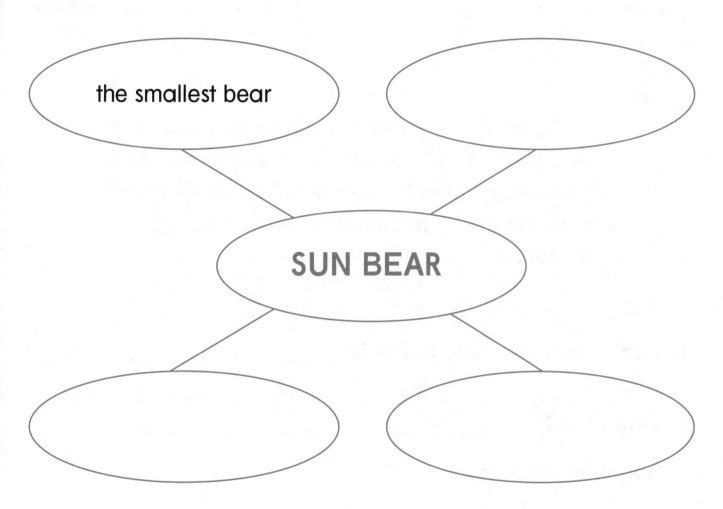

the smallest bear

SUN BEAR

Note to the Writer

Writers tell the reader about feelings. They tell you if someone in a story is sad or happy. They tell you if someone is afraid or tired.

Try This

Pretend that you are a sun bear. What kind of feelings would you have? What would make you angry? Afraid? How would you act then? Give yourself a name. Then finish each sentence.

1. I am a sun bear. My name is _____.

2. One time I _____

and was very angry.

3. When I am angry, I _____.

4. I am afraid of _____.

5. When I am afraid, I _____.

This story is about a baby panda. It has lost its mother.

A Sad Baby

Ling was very hungry. His mother always ate bamboo. Ling tried to eat some. But it was too hard to chew. "Hu, hu, hu," Ling cried, hoping his mother would hear.

Two people in the forest heard Ling's cries. They followed the sound until they found him.

"It's a baby panda! I wonder where his mother is," said the woman.

The man said, "She can't be near. She would have answered him. We had better take him with us."

Ling did not even try to run away. He was too sad and hungry. The people took him to a strange place. They gave him some milk in a bottle. Ling could drink that by himself. He also ate some apples, carrots, and soft rice.

Ling fell asleep. When he woke up, he saw another strange thing. He saw other pandas! Ling watched them from behind a tree. They looked just like him. They had heavy black and white fur. They were round and fat.

Later, the people came out of the houses. The other pandas were not afraid. The people gave them food. Finally, Ling started feeling better.

Understanding the Story

Here are some questions about the story that you just read. Read each one. Then fill in the circle beside the best answer. If you are not sure, go back and look at the story again.

■ 1.   What color is a panda's fur?

   Ⓐ   dark brown

   Ⓑ   brown and white

   Ⓒ   light brown

   Ⓓ   black and white

● 2.   Ling was sad because he was

   Ⓔ   cold   Ⓖ   sick

   Ⓕ   hungry   Ⓗ   small

■ 3.   Who found Ling?

   Ⓐ   some people

   Ⓑ   his mother

   Ⓒ   his father

   Ⓓ   a dog

★4. Pandas do not eat meat. So you can tell that **bamboo** is a kind of

(E) bird

(F) bug

(G) plant

(H) fish

■ 5. Why couldn't Ling eat the bamboo?

(A) It was too hard to chew.

(B) He couldn't find any.

(C) He liked apples better.

(D) The people wouldn't let him.

★6. What do you think the people will do with Ling now?

(E) Put him back and let him go hungry.

(F) Take care of him until he is grown.

(G) Kill him for his fur.

(H) Keep him in a cage.

Summing Up

Look at the circles. One tells things about a baby panda. The other tells about grown pandas. The colored part shows how the baby panda and the grown panda are alike. The white parts show how they are different. Fill in some facts in the white parts.

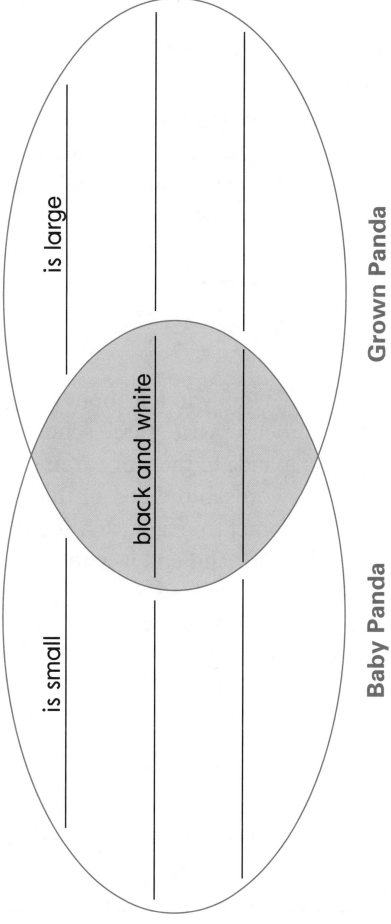

is large

is small

black and white

Grown Panda

Baby Panda

Note to the Writer

Writers tell the reader how things look. They tell you what color things are. They tell you what size and shape things are. They also tell you what things do.

Try This

Can you tell about things? On the lines below, write three sentences to tell about the panda in the story. You can use some of the words in the box or think of your own. Don't forget to begin each sentence with a capital letter and end it with a period.

| black and white | furry | round | big |
| playful | fat | eat | bamboo |

1. _____

2. _____

3. _____

Thinking About the Stories

Think about the stories you have read in this part of the book. What do you remember about sloth bears, sun bears, and pandas? Here are some questions about them. Fill in the circle beside the best answer for each one. If you are not sure, go back and look at the stories again.

● 1. How are all three bears alike?

Ⓐ They are all very mean.

Ⓑ They all have fur and eat plants.

Ⓒ They are all black and white.

Ⓓ They all eat bamboo.

● 2. How is a sun bear different from the other bears?

Ⓔ It is very slow.

Ⓕ It has no teeth.

Ⓖ It sleeps in trees.

Ⓗ It is not a bear.

● 3.   How is the sloth bear different from the other bears?

   Ⓐ   Part of its fur is black.

   Ⓑ   Sometimes it hangs upside down.

   Ⓒ   It likes honey.

   Ⓓ   It has babies.

■ 4.   Which is the smallest bear that you read about?

   Ⓔ   pandas   Ⓖ   sloth bears

   Ⓕ   sun bears   Ⓗ   baby bears

● 5.   How is the panda different from the other bears?

   Ⓐ   It has fur.

   Ⓑ   It is big.

   Ⓒ   It eats bamboo.

   Ⓓ   It gets hungry.

● 6.   How are the sun bear and the sloth bear alike?

   Ⓔ   They look the same.

   Ⓕ   They each have a mark on their chest.

   Ⓖ   They both have long hair.

   Ⓗ   They can both see well.

Summing Up

Look at the chart. At the top, there are some facts about bears. Down the side are the names of the bears. Put a + in the box if the fact is true about that bear. Put a — if it is not. The first boxes are done for you.

	is smallest	lives in Asia	eats bugs
Sloth Bear	—		
Sun Bear	+		
Panda	—		

Note to the Writer

When you write a letter, you tell people how you feel.

Try This

First circle the name of the bear that you liked best. Then write a letter to your teacher. Tell why you liked that bear the best. Write your teacher's name at the start of the letter and your name at the end.

sloth bear   **sun bear**   **panda**

Dear _____,

I liked the _____ bear best. I liked it because

_____

_____

_____

Your student,

_____